By Robert Darrol Shanks Jr., PhD

Copyright © 2025 Robert Darrol Shanks Jr. PhD

Published by: Writers Publishing House

Printed in the United States

ISBN: 978-1-64873-554-7

To The Reader

This series of short stories was a fun project to entertain my wild imagination. I used to teach English and literature years ago as a public school junior high teacher. I taught seventh, eighth and ninth grade at R.J. Barr Junior High in Grand Island, Nebraska teaching English, journalism, and special education.

I grew up in Nebraska and served in the United States Air Force (USAF) for four years as well as being a part of the Nebraska Air National Guard (ANG). After my four years serving in the Air Force as an enlisted individual, I attended college in Nebraska using the G.I. Bill obtaining my Bachelor's, Master's, and Doctor of Philosophy degrees in education from the University of Nebraska colleges located in Kearney and Lincoln, Nebraska. I stayed in the military by serving in the Nebraska Air National Guard utilizing the guard's educational assistance programs for those pursuing a higher education. I was commissioned as an Air Force officer in 1980 while still serving in the Nebraska Air National Guard. I transferred to the Air Force Reserve after moving to Arizona.

Contents

- I was fortunate to have been selected as a professor and to teach at the USAF Air War College serving as the reserve advisor to the Dean, retiring from the Air Force and reserve component in 2001. After moving to Prescott, Ariona, I also served as a part time adjunct professor for Northern Arizona University (NAU) and Embry-Riddle Aeronautical University (ERAU) here in Prescott, Arizona.

- I consider myself an Evangelical. The National Association of Evangelicals, NAE/Life Way Research, includes these statements to which respondents must agree to be categorized as evangelical:

The Bible is the highest authority for what they believe.

It is particularly important for me personally to encourage non-Christians to trust Jesus Christ as their Savior.

Jesus Christ's death on the cross is the only sacrifice that could remove the penalty of sin.

Only those who trust in Jesus Christ alone as their Savior receive God's gift of eternal salvation.

I can't emphasize enough how important my walk in Christianity has been to me and my family. Our love for Jesus Christ, our trust in Him and all that He has done for humanity is amazing. I'm also ashamed of how Christianity is so often misrepresented in the United States by the media. Always take whatever issues that life has thrown at you to our Lord and Savior in prayer. A quote from the Bible that has always been close to my heart is found in Philippians 4:6-7.

"Do not be anxious about anything, but in every situation, by prayer and petition, with thanksgiving, present your request to God. And the peace of God, which transcends all understanding will guard your hearts and your minds in Christ Jesus."

Acknowledgements

This selection of short stories could not have been written without the backing of my wife and soul mate *Cindi LaSalle-Shanks*. Her encouragement in my life is invaluable. She has been my proofreader and has suggested valuable changes. We both have experienced horrible family losses of children and have depended on each other so very much in some very difficult times.

Of course, my children are all so supportive, *Krystal Lynne Klueckman*, *Kurenia Faye Shanks*, and *Bradley Eric LaSalle*. Without such wonderful children, a father can lose sight of goals and objectives in life. This book is also dedicated to all my wonderful grandchildren and great grandchildren who are a constant delight and source of amazement. I owe a big thank you to them for helping me keep an innocence of attitude, the wonderment of discovery, the addition of current ideas and the maintenance of a positive view of life through Christianity.

This book is dedicated to the memory of our four deceased children, *Robert Scott Shanks*, *Kandace Leigh Shanks-Tettleton*, *Steven Allan LaSalle*, and *Diana Lynn LaSalle-Hontz*.

Chapter One:

A Haunted and Strange Nebraska Cornfield

Eli was a hard-working Nebraska farmer; he lived alone but had plans to find a suitable wife to share his dreams on his 180-acre farm. Eli was proud of his very productive land nestled just south of the beautiful Nebraska sand hills. His land had wonderfully thick black soil, about anything could grow in it.

After toiling one day plowing up one of his empty fields for over 12 hours, he was driving his old John Deere tractor slowly back to park it next to his barn when he saw a strange eerie light glowing in his cornfield. It was late in July, and the corn was over seven feet high already. He wondered what was that light, was it the start of a fire? He didn't have anything flammable on his tractor that would burn in the hot humid Nebraska summer air. His tractor was not leaking fuel and was running well. He had not been in that field for a long

1

time. What could be causing this strange light, he knew it could not be a fire as it had a strange green-blue glow? He needed to get out there and investigate. The summer evening light was fading fast so it would be dark soon and there was no moon this time of the month. Jumping off his tractor he rushed over to his small motorcycle to drive out quickly to investigate. The closer he got to the field the light seemed to move from one row to the next row, never letting him get close enough to see what it was. Could it be some of those wild young kids doing a prank his neighbor to the south Elmer had hired to help clean up his main farmyard? They were full of mischievous energy and behavior; Elmer had to keep them under close supervision.

Suddenly, in the fading evening sky, Eli saw a large round silver saucer shaped aircraft slowly descending above the light. He stopped his cycle and shut it down fearfully watching this round hovering machine as it slowly stopped about ten feet above the glowing cornfield. A red beam of light shot out of the craft filling the cornfield with a red glow as a small cylinder slowly levitated up to the ship disappearing into it. Just as suddenly as the UFO appeared, it shot straight up into the darkening sky and disappeared. Eli was sitting on his motorcycle in stunned silence. Racing through his mind were countless questions; what had he just seen? What was that strange greenish blue cylinder glowing in his cornfield? How did it get there and why? Are these visitors from another world? Should he report this to the local police or not? Was this a military flying device of some kind?

Breaking the warm summer evening silence suddenly was his cell phone ringing in his pocket. It was his neighbor Elmer; he had seen the unidentified flying object (UFO) as well. As he talked on the phone to Elmer, he discovered his neighbor was extremely interested in, as he called them, unidentified aerial phenomena (UAP). That was a real surprise to Eli, he had always thought

Elmer lived, ate, and slept farming and growing crops, which was all he ever talked about with Eli.

Early the next morning, Eli's phone was ringing nonstop. The local paper called and wanted to know what was going on at his farm as there were many phone calls to the paper about strange lights in the sky. The regional television station even called Eli; how did they find out what happened? Eli did not say much about the incident, only that he saw it too but gave no additional information for fear he would be swamped with unwanted visitors. His farm was only fifteen miles from town. The TV station said they could send out a crew to film things in the evening if given permission. Eli flatly refused, as there is nothing to see here and besides the fact that the TV station is 150 miles away, it would be a wasted trip, was Eli's response.

That evening, Eli stayed up late surveying the night sky hoping to see if there would be more strange flying objects above his farm. All that he could see was a brilliant Milky Way and a sky filled with stars and an occasional shooting star or meteorite.

About eight o'clock someone was at his door. It was a reporter with a film crew in tow. He wanted to know if he could get permission to set up his film crew for the evening and where would be the best spot. Eli reluctantly agreed and let him set up about a mile away on a small hill overlooking the farm and valley where Eli's farm is located. Eli told them it would be a wasted evening as nothing usually ever happens except some coyote howling and roaming javelinas. That would become an understatement for the evening!

About midnight, there was still no moon, so it was very dark in the rolling hills of Eli's farm except for a strange humming sound coming from the dark night skies. Eli was on his back deck scanning the skies when he noticed another saucer shaped UAP was sighted in the distant stars slowly moving down over the farm. This one was huge, about the size of a football field. It had a light on the top and strange lights around the outside of it and except for the faint hum it was silent. He wondered if the TV crew was alert and awake and filming this? If so, Eli would now be the center of the state's news media if the film crew caught any of this craft as the weird UAP slowly and silently descended.

The UAP went right to the same cornfield where it had been before and hovered in the same spot and again a red beam shot down into the ground in that same spot that had glowed before. What was it looking for? The craft stayed there for a short while and then again suddenly shot straight up and out of sight.

Eli again got on his motorcycle and rushed out to that field and ran down the corn row to that spot, the ground there was glowing red and was warm to the touch despite the cool evening temperatures. Sticking out of the ground was a plate made of an unknown metal with strange markings on it. What did they mean? What was the purpose of leaving this there?

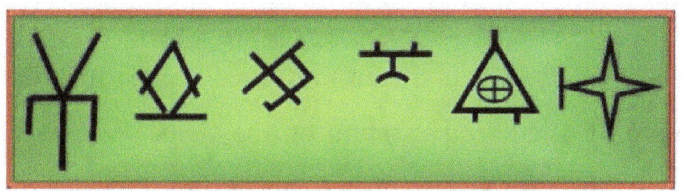

In the following weeks and months no one could decipher their meanings. The local news media went crazy, and Eli's farm was flooded with visitors from all over the U.S., with Military and political leaders coming and going and interviewing Eli, as did countless newspapers and media outlets. Eli had no explanations either except that once there had been something there this alien craft wanted back and came to retrieve it, but why did they return? What was that strange item that they beamed back that had this green blue glow? No one had any rational answers. As an interesting side note, in the Bible in John 14 2-6, Jesus said, *"In my father's house are many mansions."* Could this be a visitation from people that come from one of those mansions in the stars?

One curious thing though, the corn in this Nebraska field in an approximately fifteen-foot circular area around where the alien craft was sighted grew taller than the rest of the corn in the field. Each stock of corn also had twice as many ears of corn with the corn ears much bigger than the harvested corn not in that area of the field. The ground in that fifteen-foot circular area also had more of a radioactive return on the Geiger counter as well. The corn was evaluated and had no radioactivity and was much juicer and better than the rest of the corn from that field. To this day this strange cornfield mystery remains unsolved and unexplained.

Chapter Two

A Strange Aviation Mystery

Ross Rawlings is a highly respected entomologist researching ancient insects and a former military combat trained pilot. As he looked out the front of his small planes cockpit, none of the terrain looked familiar, yet his map and instruments all indicated he was indeed flying the proper heading and was nearing his destination according to his instruments. That was strange as he had not been airborne but for a few minutes, how could he be near his destination? As he descended to investigate, he realized he was over a jungle. He couldn't land his plane in the middle of a jungle! He increased the power to gain altitude and wondered, out loud "Where is the runway and where am I?" He had been here before many times, but now he seemed to be on the edge of a jungle, the terrain certainly didn't look like the mountains of California at all but a strange wild jungle. What's a jungle doing in the middle of the Sierra Nevada Mountains of California? Where was he actually? Ross was confused and quite bewildered. He was always taught to trust his instruments and navigation, so what is going on here? His chart and time airborne indicated Ross was just minutes from his first check point. Ross was an experienced pilot, yet this flight already had a strange feeling, his Cessna 182 had been difficult to start initially yet everything seemed alright otherwise and just after takeoff there seemed to be a strange aircraft orbiting above him as he looked out the top of the canopy. It followed him for a short time and then suddenly disappeared in a flash of light.

When Ross was preparing for his trip he had a nagging premonition that he should not go at all, this probably was from his recent research and readings about the strange occurrences of "Time Slips". Maybe his imagination was working overtime. He was quite well aware of the fact time is one of the least understood aspects of science. Was Albert Eistein correct that time and space are linked together? Suddenly there was another flash of light and now Ross was right over the runway at his destination as depicted in his chart. However, it was just a few moments ago it looked like he was right over a jungle, yet the time elapsed and charts indicated he should be coming up on his first check point. What was happening to this flight?

As he touched down and taxied over to his tie down, the mechanic in the area he knew well asked him where he had been as there were vines one would find in a jungle tangled up in his landing gear. It was a wonder the plane didn't crash into the jungle but also in the tangled vines around his landing gear was a strange dead Titan Beetle. Ross knew these huge 7-inch-long beetles live in the jungle, not the cold mountains! Ross thought he may have actually been in another place and possibly a different time, despite what his chart indicated. Another strange indication was that he had travelled over 1,000 miles to his destination in just five minutes! That was impossible but actually had happened.

His flight plan indicated he should be at his first check point. Was this a time slip? Did that mysterious aircraft that followed him have something to do with this flight? Ross was totally confused and quite shook up by this mysterious trip into the unknown.

A Titan Beetle

A Cessna 182

A Cessna over a jungle.

There have been many questions posed about alien abductions as this issue is faced by international governments. There has been some research on this phenomenon but as one delves into the subject many in the military and government leadership want this subject to just go away. Journalists have been wary about covering these events to any great extent and often just ignore the subject.

Various documentation has existed about alleged alien abductions and implants. Why has the media treated this possible alien invasion with such impunity? This could possibly be a serious national security issue. What is really going on behind closed doors in our government and military concerning this issue? Are real scientific studies being conducted concerning alien visitations? Keep an open mind about Luke's adventure in this short story.

Chapter Three:

A Tare in the Fabric of Time and Space?

 Luke was driving home from work when he noticed a strange formation in the northern Arizona sky. The sky and clouds looked like they had developed a tear similar to what one might find in a cloth fabric. Off to one side was a strange, shaped cloud he had never seen before. Little did he know he was witnessing a tear in the fabric of space and time itself and soon would be a part of an adventure he did not seek or want.

He pulled his car off to the side of the road and got out to take a quick photo when suddenly he was enveloped by a cloud like mist. The next memory is of a strange looking being standing over him, he seemed to be in a very strange room, something out of a science fiction horror story. His mind was racing, where in the world was he? He felt a sudden burning sensation in his right arm just above his hand in his wrist. He could feel something under his skin above his wrist, what was it, why was it there?

15

He slowly became aware of his surroundings and noticed the sky was not blue but wherever he was the sky was a brilliant bright green and what looked like a sun instead was a huge blue orb with a yellow halo around it. What looked like plants growing all around were pink vines with purple fruit hanging from the vines. A very tall being with a huge head and eyes of black came over to him. He was talking to Luke, but what looked like a small mouth was not moving. Luke was being communicated through his mind. The being said to eat some of the purple fruit and gave him a drink of water that had a red color, to Luke it looked like cool aid. It was very sweet. He drank a large amount as he was quite thirsty. He was still confused as he thought, "Where am I?" The being said he was on the planet Tycho in the galaxy they called Brahe. Luke said, "Why am I here?" The being said he was accidentally caught up in their cloud they used to conceal their ship. It was supposed to look like just another Earth cloud, but Luke's car was swallowed up into the mist and cloud.

Luke was starting to panic when the tall being just simply touched his arm and then he was quite calm. Luke pleaded with the being to please take him home. The being said not to worry that he will be going home soon. Suddenly the room went completely dark with the exception of a small light in the center that was aimed at Luke's head. A second entity that looked more like a robot than the tall slender individual put clamps on Lukes arms and legs and a circular band around his head. He could hear strange noises and a language he did not recognize. He felt like he was in a science fiction movie but was strangely calm.

Luke had a hearing problem and wore hearing aids, but they were gone as he placed his hand near his ear to adjust them. What was strange was he was hearing perfectly well without the aids, which was not possible, he was nearly deaf in his one ear. He felt he must be in a dream.

Luke's next memory: it's now dark, and there is a police car just ahead of his car and an officer is shining his flashlight into Lukes face. "Are you okay, have you been drinking?" was the question the office asked Luke. Luke rarely had any alcohol, perhaps a little wine with dinner occasionally but even that was rare. Where had he been what had happened to him? His car had gone off the road and was stopped just short of hitting a tree. He assured the officer he had not been drinking. He explained that he had a minor medical problem but was okay now. He felt he didn't dare tell the officer what had happened.

He reached up again, out of habit, to adjust his hearing aids but they were really actually gone, yet he was hearing perfectly well without them. This was not right, he was nearly deaf in one ear and had a great difficulty hearing anything from that side, yet he was hearing the police officer quite clearly and both aids were gone. He asked the officer what time it was, and the officer said it was after midnight. Luke said, "What? It can't be I was just on my way home from work and it was only late afternoon." Luke had lost six hours. The officer said he could call an ambulance and take him to a hospital for a checkup, but Luke said he was alright and could make it home okay now.

For Luke, he had lost time, had recovered his hearing for some strange reason and could only remember the vivid colors of where he had been and who he had talked to even though briefly. He was reluctant to tell anyone about his experience. Had there had been a tear in the fabric of time and space?

Chapter Four:

Aaron's Interdimensional Time Travel Adventure

Before we get into Aaron's story, there needs to be a brief explanation about the physics of time and dimensions. This brief explanation can be found easily on the Internet doing Google searches. So, in the study of time and dimension in standard physics, the understanding is that time has a single dimension as it can be measured only as a single variable. Unlike spatial dimensions where there is movement in any direction, time is unique in that it only moves forward, from past to future, a concept known in science as the "arrow of time." Time and space are linked together in a four-dimensional fabric called "spacetime". Movement through this spacetime continuum, and time is the dimension that measures intervals of change. Scientific studies suggest that having more than one time dimension could result in an unstable universe. For now, the prevailing view in physics is that time, as we experience and measure it, is really just one-

dimensional and inseparable from space. Is this what Aaron is about to find out?

Aaron's hyperspace vehicle was now repaired after his narrow escape from a band of space pirates he encountered in a strange galaxy. His hyper drive became uncontrollable as it took him into a scary and wild dimension. He always read his Bible and looked for scriptures for guidance and protection before his trips into the unknown realms of the time dimension travel. His new neutrino drive was experimental and was not often used for interdimensional travel and was not recommended to be used at all due to its highly unpredictability when being engaged from the regular interstellar atomic drive to interdimensional settings.

Usually, Aaron could select a region of space he wanted to check out for possible life using his special neutrino drive selection so he could move between dimensions. This was the year 3001 so travel inter-dimensionally was now a reality but not used often due to all the special regulations, permissions, and procedures needed to travel the many unknown and uncharted dimensions of time. Few intergalactic rocketeers, known in 3001 as Time Jockeys, traveled into these uncharted and unknown dimensions using this special neutrino drive that needed not only special permission, but also highly rare earth material known as scandium. This very rare earth material is a by-product of uranium extraction and is only used primarily for aerospace components. Aaron's ship was leased out by the United Galactic Federation since his ship had the special drive needed for interdimensional travel.

If Aaron were to use his special neutrino drive without permission and following all the guidelines he could lose his license as an interstellar pilot with his ship seized and his dismissal and discharge from service as an intergalactic space pilot.

He had a lot of explaining to do to those leaders in the higher chain of command as travel to that strange galaxy was not entirely approved. The approval was working its way up the chain of command and looked as if it was going to be allowed. However, Aaron jumped the gun so to speak and used his neutrino drive anyway. He barely escaped the space pirates and had a difficult time returning with a partially disabled ship. Travel through time and dimensions was difficult with many hidden dangers. Aaron was fortunate to even get back to our solar system. He was found adrift with no engine power near the planet Mars. He was lucky to be rescued at all and was really in a lot of "hot water" with leadership.

Aaron was able to bring back a lot of photographic research and other sensor captured data. This allowed the scientists at the Federation of United Planets to examine all of the recorded information along with a host of other sensor data. Aaron had traveled to the region in space that the James Webb Telescope had detected possible molecules of life in the atmosphere of exoplanet Kepler 62e, the planet was much larger than earth. He was totally surprised at what he found and was attacked by what he assumed were space pirates judging from their hostility and use of sophisticated weaponry he had never seen before. He could not defend himself as he was unarmed with the exception of his cloaking device which he used

Earth Kepler-62 e

to escape. He had installed the cloaking device over a period of one year as he acquired the parts and technology. He was in trouble for that as well as he did not have permission to acquire that technology and use it, however that was what saved his life and ship. He was a rebellious hero in a lot of trouble.

Chapter Five:

Lost in a Time Slip

First of all, just what is a "Time Slip"? Jessica Schrader, writing in [1]Psychology Today wrote an article on Time Slips:

In her article she makes it quite clear that the nature of time is one of the biggest mysteries in science. Scientists simply do not understand just what time really is.

Time anomalies or slips in time to another era have

been reported by many over the years, the Internet is filled with these stories whether one believes them or not. While time travel is not really possible some interstellar space jockeys have reported strange "time slips" or time anomalies. They have been

---

[1] (Time-slips-the-multiverse-and-you, n.d.)

characterized as paranormal episodes by some psychologists. Over a 100 years ago Albert Einstein's theory was that time and space are linked together and that nothing can travel faster than the speed of light. However, there are countless stories about people experiencing strange encounters with strange shifts in time.

A person or group of folks have reported traveling through time without knowing why it was occurring. There was  *supposedly an account that occurred in the 1970's in Oklahoma when three cattlemen were herding some cattle on a ranch when they noticed a strange white house on a hill. Since they had never seen it there before they came back the next day to investigate and while the hill was still there, the house was now gone. All three ranch hands said they saw it. Did it really exist in a different moment in time just to be briefly seen by the ranchers? Was this a time slip?*

Captain Caspian Vale had heard many stories about "Time Slips" before and even though traveling close to the speed of light was now a reality the actual speed of light was not thought to be attainable by many scientists even though the Hyper Drive's maximum speed was not far from the speed of light (186,000 miles per second). He thought these stories of people slipping into another realm of time to be possible fantasies, or nightmares people had experienced. He always tried to keep an open mind, but he also understood that there are unknown anomalies in the understanding of time. Even in Captain Vales' era the concept of time and space and how they were linked together was still not fully understood by science.

So, when he engaged his Hyper Drive, it gave him a start as the ship jumped into interstellar flight. Flying close to the speed of light was indeed frightening and few were allowed to even use this drive due to strict Space Federation rules and guidelines because it was strictly regulated and highly classified. The amount of energy theorized to reach the speed of light was also unattainable. So, flying close to the speed of light was indeed frightening and many space pilots never really got used to engaging the Hyper Drive, even if allowed by the Orwellian controlled Space Federation. Coming out of

Hyper Drive was just as scary, one always had the fear of being somewhere unintended and now stranded forever. What if Captain Vale was accidentally caught in a Time Slip and didn't realize it? According to the Captain, this is apparently what happened to him on a recent flight from Earth to the distant planet of Pluto. As he was engaging his ship's Hyper Drive there was a flash of light, and he suddenly found himself still in stationary orbit around the Earth instead. However, something was amiss, there were no satellites, no space station at all in orbit and the Earth looked almost too pristine. He tried to access the known Space Federation communications networks but there was nothing but silence. In fact, there were no communication networks of any kind detected. Was this the Earth he had just left? Was this another Earth in a parallel dimension?

He decided to take his small exploration saucer shaped ship used to access in-orbit supplies from the International Space station to investigate. The little ship was easy to fly, and this seemed like a very much needed low level surveillance flight. What he was able to see was simply astonishing. He was flying over what appeared to be a medieval village in what should have been the large bustling city of Kersey, England located in Suffolk County. There were no people, no TV aerials, no telephone, or light wires. The houses looked extremely ancient. At the stream were ducks but they looked lifeless almost like decoys. He was able to beam onto his ship the remnants of an old Morning London newspaper, the Standard, lying in the street, it had the date of 1857 on it.

There seemed to be no sign of any habitation. It seemed like a ghost city.

After returning to the main ship there was another flash of light and Captain Vale was back in his stationary Earth orbit above modern-day England. He had just engaged his Hyper Drive to leave on his trip to the outer edge of the solar system only what seemed like minutes before. He reported the strange malfunction of his Hyper Drive to the Operations Center. They reported he had disappeared from radar and then suddenly reappeared having been gone for less than five minutes. He said his ship's chronometer indicated he was gone for over two hours!

His operations commander was simply astonished at the digital recording that was on his small operational craft of what appeared to be an old medieval village. No one could explain what had happened as detected in the short visual recording. Captain Vale's physical proof, the remnant of the ancient 1857 Standard London newspaper just suddenly disappeared as he returned to his normal time frame. He suddenly became a believer in "Time Slips". In his mind that was the only logical conclusion he could reach about this unexplained event in time.

Chapter Six:

The Forgotten Time Machine

The Amazon is not a place to get lost in and has many dangerous animals and insects, but Silas Maximillan and his crew kept slogging along cutting the undergrowth as they went. The humidity was stifling and tasked everyone's energy to the limit. They were following an old tale discovered stuck in an old Spanish book about the early days of discovery in Brazil. The old document was folded up and difficult to open but working diligently in the lab Wilson Reynolds, a document expert had slowly opened it using the many techniques he had perfected over the years to save old parchment. The tattered document had been found in a small antique shop in Recife, Brazil.

As the researchers deciphered the old note it said, the Lost City of Z was closer than many thought and was well hidden under the thick Amazon growth but could be easily accessed through a small tunnel. Everyone wondered, "What tunnel? No tunnels had been found in that region of the Amazon according to local history.

Using Light Detection and Ranging (LIDAR) modern archeologists were finding many unknown human habitation and ancient cities that once existed in the Amazon region. Along with ancient tribes being discovered, archeologists in July of 2024, found an isolated native group of people known as the Mashco Piro tribe living in the Amazon near Peru. This ancient tribe had no prior documented contact with the outside world. In August of 2025, another isolated tribe in the Massaco region was also discovered. Large areas of the Amazon combined with its remoteness and lack of infrastructure makes most regions of the Amazon extremely difficult to access. There are no roads, so it is impossible to move about freely. Many biologists have postulated that there are countless plants and species still waiting to be discovered and identified. This team looking for a possible tunnel had many obstacles to overcome.

Part of Maximillan's crew was Ross Rawlings a noted entomologist who hoped to discover and begin to categorize unknown insects, flora, and fauna. According to the ancient document there are large flat-topped mountains with caves and cliffs in the area known as Tepuis or Sky Islands but are hidden by the dense forest growth. Perhaps there is a hidden tunnel in that area. These ancient and isolated tabletop mountains rise abruptly from the Amazon rainforest and have unique ecosystems with a variety of species found nowhere else on Earth.

At the heart of this expedition is the Amazon River that has been low during drought conditions the last decade and has plagued the area where the team was hoping to find this mysterious tunnel in the thick vegetation. In 2023 the low water levels exposed ancient rock carvings thought to be thousands of years old and fits in with the brief cryptic note about the lost city of Z. Ancient floodplains have hidden some of these archaeological sites and ancient human settlements but now these newly discovered areas have given the team a lot of valuable information.

Silas was interested in one particular mountain jutting up out of the Amazon, it is known as the Snoring Mountain due to the sound the wind makes against the rock faces, caves, and cliffs in that central region. He had often said perhaps the supposed tunnel was near that mountain hidden in the deep underbrush of the Amazon. The team was headed that way, but the trek was unbelievably slow due to the thick jungle under growth, lots of insects and other dangerous animals and plants they had to be wary of contacting. He had often theorized that underneath the surface of the Amazon basin was a massive structural depression filled in over millions of years with sedimentary layers with rare rock outcrops, however, many valuable rocks had been discovered there over the years leading to trade and some mining. However, the rainforest is under attack from illegal and unchecked development from agricultural expansion, logging and other illegal mining activities causing damage to the forest. With all of this in mind Silas and his team were being very careful and respectful as they moved to the interior. The native porters hired were very helpful with information and methods as they hacked their way into the interior.

At one point, one of the porters just disappeared leaving his back pack hanging on the edge of a large hole he had fallen into. He was rescued and very traumatized by falling into a deep twenty-foot hole but was otherwise okay. Further checking showed this was indeed part of a winding deep tunnel like depression. The question arose; is this the tunnel mentioned in the old parchment document?

As more jungle debris was removed and the area leveled off the team saw a faint metal like shine deeper into the depression. As they cleared away the undergrowth it looked like a round capsule-like affair. Ropes were carefully lowered and wrapped around the strange metal looking capsule and slowly hoisted up to ground level. The capsule was about twelve feet in diameter and very light for its size and had what looked like a small door-like opening on one side. As they tried to open it the door-like area seemed sealed with what looked like a small handle at one side. As the team tinkered with the handle-like protrusion, the door suddenly popped open, opening with a loud hiss as the trapped air inside hissed out with a strange odor.

The team was alarmed and puzzled, as they peered in with their flash lights to a strange looking instrument panel with a language in a small plate in the center of the instruments none of them had ever seen before. The porters became alarmed and just ran away leaving all they were carrying strung out over the ground. There were two seats in the capsule, and they were quite small, almost child-like in size. One human could probably fit into this round silver orb if they weren't too large.

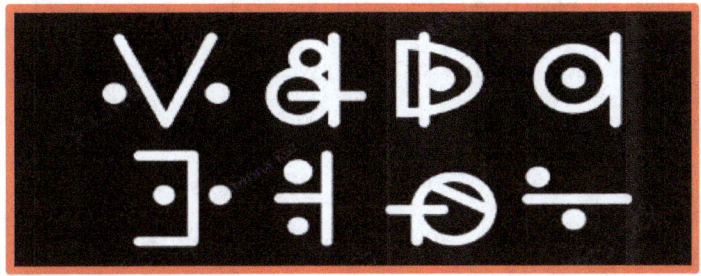

Nothing like this had ever been found before and so intact. Immediately the team notified the proper individuals in the chain of command. A complete blackout of radio communications was ordered, and the device was covered and moved so it could be transported to a laboratory for closer examination. Everyone was sworn to a high level of secrecy as the device was loaded up onto a make shift trailer on a roughly hewn road leading out of the Amazon. Any radio discussions were disguised in a host of code words that would be meaningless to anyone listening to the conversations.

Silas was sure this was not made by any humans, the technology they were seeing in the inside was made of materials never before seen. The entire capsule weighed less than 1500 pounds. The metal was extremely light and reminded some of the team of what was supposedly discovered in 1947 in Roswell, New Mexico of a crashed UFO. Much of this capsule was indeed strange and amazing. How did it get there and why was it buried and not damaged in any way? One theory discussed was that it could be some kind of a time machine, but what happened to the occupants? Were they rescued by another UFO or did they perish in the hostile Amazon jungle environment?

Back at the laboratory in an undisclosed state in the U.S., technicians and scientists were going over the capsule closely. Once they were able to figure out how to get some power to it the instrument panel lit up and looked like it was operational. One smaller scientist was manipulating the various switches in the instrument panel when suddenly the entire capsule just disappeared taking the unsuspecting scientist with it. It suddenly reappeared again in the laboratory just where it had been. The capsule was damp and had a strange smell about it.

The unsuspecting technician said, "What happened to me?" He asked what year it was and looked much older. He said he had been gone for a very long time and had a full growth of beard; his clothes were tattered as well. He said the world he saw was completely different with strange small gray beings that seemed to understand him by just reading his mind. They didn't wear clothes like we do and had a variety of flying disc type aerial vehicles we would call "flying saucers". Their world was completely different according to him. He was very confused and was questioned closely about what had happened and where he had been. He needed counseling and was hospitalized for a complete physical examination. He appeared to be in good health, he said he survived on a strange fruit grown on wild looking trees. The "grays" through apparently mental telepathy said the fruit was good and would not hurt him. Why the capsule returned was a complete mystery, perhaps it was merely a suggestion that there are other worlds out there to be discovered, and the scientist should be returned to his world and correct time.

The scientific team was working to reverse engineer some of the devices in the capsule and figure out how and why they worked. The entire project was now highly classified with a strict "need to know" basis for those working on the Amazon capsule.

Chapter Seven:

The Blacksmith

Seth was a popular and well-liked Blacksmith who was very community minded and quite patriotic and curious, traits that could benefit him well but also could get him into trouble during this tumultuous Revolutionary time in the colonies. He was charged with the job of forging arms for the Minute Men but also making and repairing tools, not only for the locals but also for the British regiment stationed in the area.

 Today his forge was abnormally hot with no air circulating despite his two large doors being open. Rushing into Seth's shop were a number of patriot volunteers unloading six brass cannon that the British had spiked; this practice is used when abandoning artillery by pounding a metal plug

into the cannon's touch hole the breech near the rear of the barrel where the charge could be ignited. Spiking prevented the cannon from being used.

Seth was certain all of the cannon could be repaired. For the next six weeks, working day and night, all of the cannon were repaired. The cannon were then used during the Siege of Boston that lasted nearly a year from April of 1775 until March of 1776. The British finally abandoned Boston. Because of Seth's efforts he became a local hero.

Shortly after that British force retreated and left, another smaller force was dispatched to confiscate and destroy any patriot arms and ammunition and recover some stolen British cannon. The British force searched Seth's workshop and quizzed him relentlessly as to what he knew of the missing cannon. He of course said he knew nothing. The small British force was commanded by Lt. Colonel Frances Smith, and they did not bring any cannon. They also were searching for cannon stolen from the British armory. The colonial militia knew the British were coming so Seth and his crew were able to move and hide any arms they had been working on and repairing.

American 'rebels' hounded the British during their retreat back to Boston, firing at them from behind stone walls and trees. Throughout the war, Seth continued to help repair firearms. He also made ammunition cartridges. One story told says that on one occasion, when he ran out of flannel to wrap the charges, he cut up and used his own clothing. He was always ready to visit the sick, especially among the families of soldiers, improving upon his knowledge and skill he had acquired from his mother and family using herbs and roots to help the sick and wounded.

Local British law was very harsh, they did not permit the creation or use of most iron products, but Seth and other colonial blacksmiths simply ignored the rules and continued to produce the tools and weapons needed that eventually contributed to the new country of America's independence.

Early American history has many stories of bravery in the face of difficult control by the occupying force of British soldiers. There is much to learn about our early colonial Americans bravery and struggle that eventually made America what is today. American educators have a tremendous amount of textbooks and information for their American history classes.

When reading about American history it is important to realize what it was like to live in that time and not place current beliefs and political bias on our history. All Americans must guard against the dilution and attempts to twist and alter history to fit current political issues.

What our country is experiencing now politically should have no effect on how we understand our past history, we must all read it and place it in a proper perspective in our minds. The greatness of our country is due to the tough and fearless early Americans to remain free and flourish, to fight for what is right and to continue to support our Constitution and Bill of Rights. These documents should be taught and understood by all citizens, the basis for our great country. Learn them as they are written. Realize the importance of our

Constitution and Bill of Rights to our freedoms we experience and take for granted every day.

We all must resist any efforts to minimize, unfairly criticize, and distort these wonderful documents. These documents are what makes the USA one of the greatest countries in the world! [2]

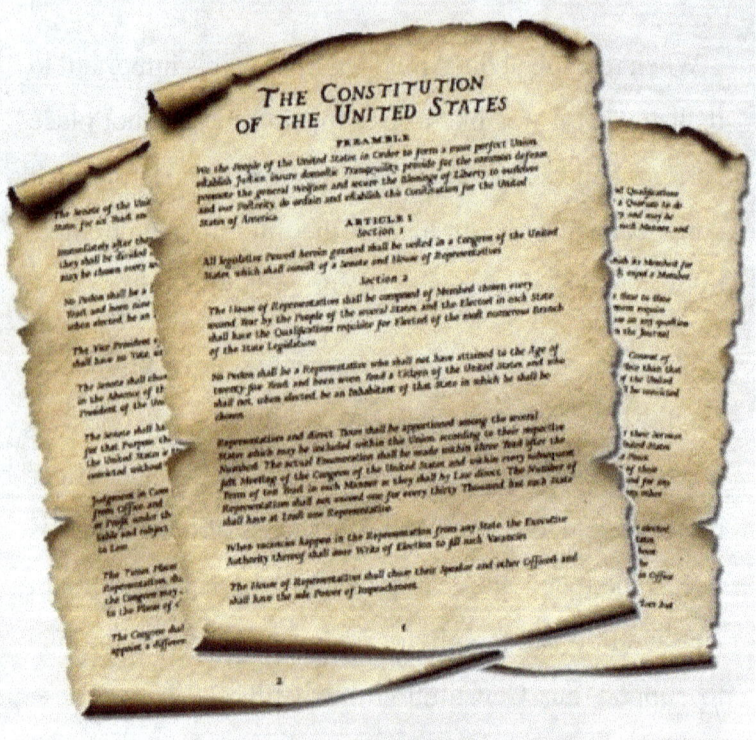

[2] (Blacksmith-Ncolonial-Blacksmiths-Minutemen-Revolutionar, n.d.)

Chapter Eight:

The Massive Red Cloud

A massive red cloud descended over the entire farm and area owned by Alexander Bixby. Alex was a key member of his small farming community. He was also a rather outspoken guy and had some very narrow dogmatic views of life. He was fascinated by the night sky and spent many evenings sitting behind his telescope observing the heavens. He lived alone after his wife had suddenly passed. The unbearable pain of her loss was eased somewhat as he studied the stars each night and he remembered the wonderful old times with his wife when he first got his farm. She loved viewing the constellation Orion especially. So, Alex had a very soft spot in his heart for that special star cluster.

 One blustery evening he was braving the cold crystal-clear Nebraska winter air again studying the Orion Constellation. He was trying to visualize what it must have been like living in those ancient Greek times and wondering about the heavens. He was sipping on a hot cup of coffee and eating his left-over cold chili supper.

Suddenly, a massive red cloud began to descend on his farm. At first he thought it must be a storm moving in, the Nebraska prairie thunderstorms often came up suddenly, however, the weather forecast for the next week was clear skies and cold weather. The clear winter sky disappeared as the cloud enveloped Alex and his farm. He was momentarily stunned at the sudden weather change. At about the same time he heard a strange hum. His farm was on the border with the Nebraska sand hills and there were a lot of old stories from the local Pawnee Indians about strange beings, one was about a giant raptor called Hu-huk. There were also stories of a strange bird the pioneers who came through Nebraska had handed down. There were even ruts left in the prairie where the wagon trains came through the prairie on the way west. The Murdock wagon ruts near Alda, Nebraska are well known. The native Pawnee Indian tribes often told of the giant Raptor called Hu-huk that would terrorize local farmers so was this hum and red cloud related to those stories or was his imagination running wild?

It was disconcerting and worrisome as the hum seemed to get worse during the night. The red cloud was not part of the sunset either. Alex was getting concerned so he called his neighbor Levi. Levi was also worried as was his wife, she was getting upset as the hum was intensifying and painful to her sensitive hearing.

 About as suddenly as the cloud descended and the annoying hum started; it stopped. The sudden quietness was in

itself almost as bad as the hum. Alex was terrified and for a moment and didn't know what to do if anything.

About the time the hum stopped there was a blood curdling screech as a large birdlike creature swooped down over Alex and then suddenly disappeared in the low hanging red mist. As the creature disappeared the sky suddenly cleared as the rising sun slowly warmed up the cold Nebraska air.

Chapter Nine

Quantum Entanglement in a Far Away Galaxy

There is a lot of research taking place on this topic so just what is Quantum Entanglement?

Quantum entanglement is one of the most intriguing, and also misunderstood, phenomena in physics. The concept is a complex physics theory the average citizen won't understand or probably care about. Albert Einstein, in a letter to Max Born in 1947, referred to it saying: "I cannot seriously believe in it because the theory cannot be reconciled with the idea that physics should represent a reality in time and space, free from spooky action at a distance" Quantum entanglement describes a special connection between particles. It is a quantum mechanical phenomenon at the quantum level, where the quantum states of two particles must be described with reference to each other, even if these particles are spatially separated. The properties of one particle become instantaneously affected by measurements conducted on the other, so they are then co-dependent. Suppose you have a pair of socks in two separate gift boxes. If you open one and see it is the left sock, you instantly know the other box contains the right sock—even if it's on the other side of the world!

Proximus Centauri (Hubble Photo)

Captain Miles Crawford had just come out of a special worm hole transporting him and his space ship to a galaxy 4 light years away from Earth known as Proximus Centauri. A possible Earth-like planet was discovered there with the possibility it may contain some form of life due to some special instrumentation developed to detect possible life. Travel at and above the speed of light, also known as superluminal travel, was now available for deep space flights.

Captain Crawford was also using a new communication system based on quantum entanglement research and development. The Space Federation had pioneered a new system using two radios with a special channel for communicating via the spooky concept that the special physics needed to adjust to the space time connections was now using two special communication frequencies known as QE time dilation where the reality of time and space is compressed despite the vast distances separating them. Communication was now instantaneous. Alcubierre (Al-koo-byair) Warp drive travel to other galaxies was now possible using a newly discovered and synthesized rare earth negative energy matter known as Einsteinium. This new element prevents worm holes (they are basically unstable) from collapsing. Einsteinium makes worm holes stable for brief periods of time, so limited deep space exploration is possible.

Captain Crawford's ship was powered using the new innovative negative energy system (anti-gravity powered) called the A-One Warp Drive engine system developed by theoretical physicist Miguel Alcubierre and based on Einstein's theory of relativity.

As the Captain surveyed the strange-looking planet below, a bright flash suddenly blinded him as the inside of his ship began to light up and glow. A voice came up in his audio and wanted to know who he was and why he was flying in sacred air space above the planet Proximus Centauri.

Before he could respond the voice said they knew all about him and his hostile planet Earth; he was ordered to leave their planet immediately, these beings could read his mind as he tried to speak. Appearing before his ship was a temporary worm hole he was immediately sucked into and returned to Earth orbit. The next thing he remembered he was in a hospital bed aboard a Space Federation hospital ship orbiting the Earth.

Captain Crawford pleaded with the doctors to let him speak to his commander, he had to warn them that using this traversable worm hole to Proximus Centuria was not recommended. These beings he only encountered by voice were far advanced by at least one thousand years to Earth's civilizations. For some reason he seemed to know more about them than he wanted.

He had developed a cultural history understanding of this race living in that far away galaxy. He stated that they had been visiting and monitoring Earth for an eon and was alarmed at how war like our civilizations here on Earth are to each other. The captain said that their monitoring appearances were listed in some of Earth's history and often unidentified as flying objects called flying saucers or UFOs. They had even been depicted in some of Earth's early art history in drawings and paintings as well. He knew they had even taken some humans aboard their ships to examine why we were so violent. He knew they were often called the "grays" since they were smaller than humans and colored more neutrally in a grey color. Why the Captain knew all of this was a mystery to him, even his chain of command was concerned at the amount of information he was able to share. At one point, the doctors considered possibly that Captain Crawford may need counseling, however, much of what he shared about anti-gravity was critical and was shared with scientists in the development of new realms of space flight that were being researched. He, however, was also now looked upon as somewhat of an alarmist and almost as a scientific hermit in his thinking about future space flight. He even pointed the astronomers into new unknown regions of space that he felt needed further research.

At one point, Captain Crawford told astronomers to examine more closely the blank area of space known as "The Great Nothing." While there seemed to be few if any galaxies or stars located in this region of space, he assured the astronomers that was where the worm hole had taken him. They continued to interrogate him and wanted specific information. At one point, Captain Crawford became wary of all the negative attention. One late afternoon he asked one of his interrogators for a writing pad. He began, from memory, to jot down the exact coordinates of where two distinct monoliths had appeared. He admitted there were a lot of copy cats, over 200 worldwide, but he assured his scientific team assigned to him that these two were left purposefully by the aliens that he had encountered as a warning. The one in Wyoming, known as "The Devil's Tower," was there as the main warning. He warned against all worm hole travel to any of the cosmic

voids, but he knew his warnings would go unheeded.

As Captain Crawford retired from the Space Federation, he had taken on quite the appearance of an old sage with white hair, he also now had a very calm demeanor as well. He was affectionately known as the "Sage of Outer Space". He said to stay away from the Boötes (boh-OH-teez) Void spherical region of space thought to be millions of light years from Earth. Would the scientists heed his warning, he was doubtful? He would always be famous for all his data that led to the development of the anti-gravity engines for deep space flight.

His warning was to be wary of any monoliths that appeared in areas where they shouldn't be and to research them carefully!

Chapter Ten:

Hypersonics Gone Awry

Colonel Simeon Darrol knew he was testing a highly sensitive aircraft for the Department of War and the United States Air Force, but it had to be done so he volunteered to test fly this new hypersonic powered vehicle using a new miniature specially powered atomic scram jet engine. He would be flying above Mach 5 for a short time and knew the molecules in the air begin to vibrate and break apart at that speed. He also knew that above Mach 10 the atoms can become ionized, creating a charged plasma sheath around the vehicle. When this happens, the air flowing around the hypersonic vehicle can behave in unique and unpredictable ways. The shock layer air between the vehicle and the shockwave it is creating can become very thin with high temperature increases and can threaten the aircraft's stability and control. Wind tunnel tests had shown this aircraft highly unstable in certain conditions but that was only a wind tunnel test. What would happen in reality?

Colonel Darrol was pushing his aircraft to the limit following all the test parameters set up for this test, but he didn't expect what was about to happen to him. He was fully suited up in a space-like suit when the aircraft entered a tunnel like affair as the titanium alloy making up the front of the aircraft began to vibrate and turn a strange blue color. His aircraft just disappeared from radar as he approached Mach 7.5 as he entered what was later to be called the "tunnel of time."

Apparently, the flight test exceeded the limit of Mach 7.5 and because the vehicle had exceeded the flight parameters of Mach 7.5. The atoms had become ionized causing the aircraft to enter a high-speed time tunnel, it had created its own charged plasma sheath around the vehicle resulting in the aircraft becoming the first ionized

59

"high speed" hypersonic time machine. The air flowing around the hypersonic vehicle caused an unknown and unpredictable "time tunnel" to form, a unique alteration of space and time due to an unknown, and at this point, an unexplainable Hypersonics anomaly.

The next thing he knew he was landing on a very unusual runway, it looked like it was made out of ice, and it was on a very cold and windy area, and it was an airport he had never seen before. The buildings looked like they were all made out snow. Instead of a blue sky the air and sky was a green color with clouds overhead that looked like pink puffs of pink cotton candy. His aircraft's chronometer said it was now the year 2140. What was going on here? It was 2026 and the Air Force was here at area 51 as the flight leader in testing this new atomic scram jet engine.

As soon as he landed, his aircraft was surrounded by odd looking vehicles that said they were part of the National Socialists of North Americus Security Forces. Where was the Colonel? He was testing this aircraft at the Area 51 Groom Lake Test Facility in Nevada. What country is North Americus, he had never heard of that before and what happened to all the high desert landing areas of Area 51? Why was it so bitterly cold and what were all of these buildings that looked like they were made out of snow? All the aircraft parked along the buildings had the appearance of flying saucers.

The individuals in the odd security vehicles surrounded the aircraft, they were all blue colored and had weird antenna type affairs sticking out of their heads, their eyes were all black and very large. They were pointing what appeared to be weapons of some kind at his aircraft.

He was told in a language he had never heard before and through telepathy in English that he was being arrested for flying an unauthorized aircraft and landing it at a highly restricted space port used just for alien pilots coming in to this alternate dimension called Terra Cosmos. Again, through telepathy he was told he was not allowed to travel through time and would also be charged with a time dilation violation. Time travel was possible but not permitted in this alternate dimension. Colonel Darrol was totally confused and demanded to see whoever was in charge of this facility. Time travel, although it now existed, was not permitted or allowed in this very socialistic controlled alternate dimension. He felt like he was in a George Orwell socialist/communistic dimension of some type.

Apparently Colonel Darrol was told he was now in another alternate dimension due to his flying at speeds above Mach 5 in an unauthorized time machine that was in an aircraft configuration. He tried to explain he was a special test pilot flying for the United States Air Force and again, through telepathy, he simply said he just wanted to go back to his proper time frame if somehow he had traversed time accidently, if that was what had happened. The main Officer in Charge of the facility Comrade Stalinsky said he would see what could be done, at least it seemed he was cooperative and wanted to resolve this problem.

Colonel Darrol, along with his disassembled aircraft was placed in a special sealed device and suddenly he was back at Area 51. Fire trucks, ambulances, and crash trucks descended on the rather confused pilot sitting amid his disassembled aircraft along the dry lake bed.

At the debriefing he tried to explain what had happened, as unbelievable as it was, and the result that this test was immediately reclassified as highly classified so it could be completely studied and researched as part of a special time travel research concept. Colonel Darrol was examined completely and found to be in excellent condition and sworn to complete secrecy, he was never to speak of what happened to him.

Chapter Eleven:

Ley Lines, the Invisible Electronic Energy Grid

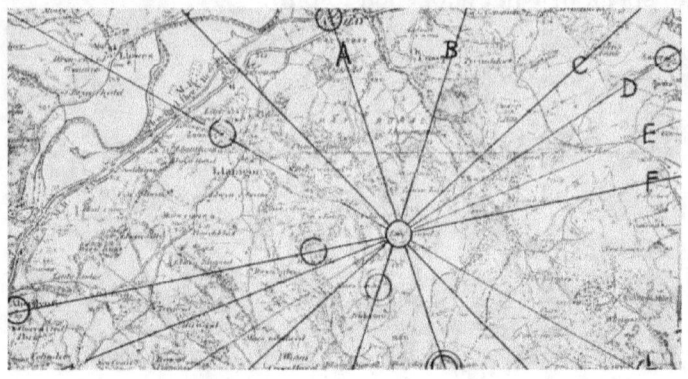

James had experienced the mysterious unwanted electronic power of the so-called Ley Lines when he as a youth hiking in the high mountains of Colorado. His phone would suddenly erupt as an unwanted cascade of energy engulfed it. He really preferred a paper map and charts and always preferred them; he had a severe dislike for the electronic maps displayed on his phone and lap top computer. All he wanted was to simply jot down notes on the map and keep if folded up in his back pack. The mass of extraneous energy that was being emitted from the countless electronic devices everyone now seemed to be carrying was really, as he called it, "nothing more than electronic distractions" interfering with how his mind worked.

James was a highly skilled and registered Professional Archaeologist and had done a lot of research and analysis for several universities at several Egyptian sites. He was also a renowned author, professional photographer, and journalist.

Long ago, James had discounted the theory that these invisible ley lines, like latitudinal and longitudinal lines that crisscross maps, carried supernatural energy that only a few select individuals could access and interpret. James was a good analyst and had done all the research to blow up these ideas that seemed more like fairy tales than true science. He knew the concept of ley lines had been introduced by Alfred Watkins in the 1920s, suggesting these lines were just straight pathways used mainly for navigation and knew that using a map and drawing a straight line between two points was over simplifying navigation. Watkins didn't suggest that these navigation lines had any magic or mystical properties. The lines are just simple theoretical lines used to connect landmarks, however, some so called "New Age" proponents were trying to convince "wana be" academics they had special sacred energies connecting Stonehenge and the Pyramids of Giza despite the fact there didn't exist any scientific data supporting this idea. Most academic archaeologists along with university level scientific research clearly indicated any cluster of ancient sites can appear aligned if enough data points are selected.

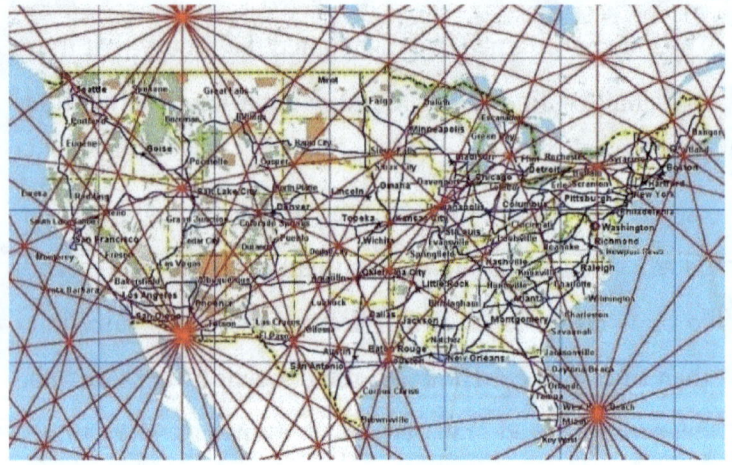

James was interested in one ley line that seemed to start at the Giza pyramids and then suddenly end in the middle of the Amazon jungle. As he traced this and examined it closely he noticed that this area of the Amazon jungle had been thoroughly scanned by the Light Detecting and Ranging Radar (LIDAR) where it looked like some ancient buildings and a possible civilization had developed this entire area. LIDAR removes all types of clutter that can interfere with the scan.

As he investigated in more detail he discovered some key scientists were working on a possible trip to this deep in the Amazon site to do more of a detailed archaeological analysis. He knew some of them and was going to contact the one he knew best to see if he could be included in the expedition as this was what he loved to do and had extensive and detailed experiences in Egypt at many of the ancient sites there.

His latest book, "How to Treat Scientists with the Stupidity Disease" was a best seller. He had laid bare the new age movement and in particular the so-called Cosmic Evolutionary Optimism that mankind was moving toward a new order of enlightenment and consciousness, a fringe paranormal theory about UFOs, crop circles and other Earth theories and energies that in reality didn't exist since there is no evidence indicating these theories and Earth energies exist.

James always looked at the lack of evidence wholistically. He thought more research and investigation was needed to prove or disprove a claim was false. He knew of course that many of the so-called New Age Earth mysteries and theories were nothing more than fringe beliefs with no logical data to support them. While he found the Light Cone theory interesting, it also is just an observational theory that past events are seen but if in the future they haven't happened yet so this light cone theory posits that events in the future will be seen soon but what has happened in the past has already been seen. How can this even be proved? It really can't be proved; it's just an idea of how the past and future exists.

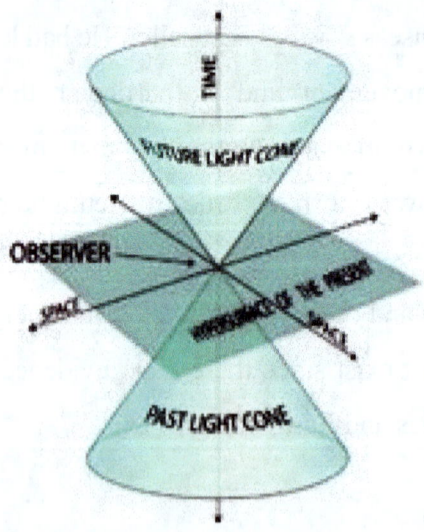

James is now part of the expedition to examine the mysterious and hard to access area of the Amazon Jungle. The expedition is to leave soon, he feels honored to be a part of this rather isolated and hard to get to Amazon jungle area but apparently a key ley line exploration and analysis of what may really be there.

Ley Lines Amazon Expedition

Setting up this Amazon Forest expedition was not an easy task for many reasons, first and foremost, the section where the Ley Line ended is the Mura Nunka Hills in Ecuador and is not been explored to any extent and is extremely difficult to even access due to the incredibly dense forest, with intersecting ecosystems making travel there difficult to nearly impossible without special military-trained special forces and equipment. There are few roads, even fewer that are even in passable condition. There are impassable rivers and rapids. The climate is extremely challenging, it is hot, humid with constant wet conditions making it a difficult and dangerous environment for humans and equipment. The Amazon's vastness is a key issue as it is approximately one-third the size of South America with little to no comprehensive mapping having ever been done.

The Ley Line ended about 200 miles almost due east of the Yasuni National Park and the city of El Coca. The team flew to the city Quito, then flew to El Coca in the Yasuni National Park. The Ley Line had ended in approximately the center of the deepest part of the Amazon Jungle then overland to the Ley Line ending coordinates. It was going to take at least three months to get to that location using the rivers when possible and cutting a trail overland to the Ley Line ending coordinates.

To get to the Amazon from Ecuador, fly from Quito to the city of **El Coca**, the primary gateway, then transfer to

a river port for a boat ride to your chosen ecolodge or cruise, typically on the **Napo River**. The Yasuni National Park lies within the Napo Rain Forest. The park is about 160 miles from Quito, Ecuador, the

Yasuni National Park

city of El Coca is the main entrance to the Amazon

Forest. What would the team find, if anything, at those Ley Line ending coordinates that were still another approximately 200 miles from the Yasuni National Park to the center of the Amazon Jungle? The Ley Line coordinates ending point were just south of the Amazon River right in the center of the Amazon Forest. There were two known uncontacted indigenous tribes in the Yasuni Park area. How many other indigenous tribes were located in those unexplored areas where the team was headed? Past experience has shown most of these tribes are suspicious of outsiders and especially of drug dealers, many were hostile to outsiders of any kind. To hack through the jungle the team would be lucky to move a quarter of a mile a day so moving down the Amazon to just north of the coordinates was the plan before hacking their way south into the jungle to the coordinates.

The team is facing dangerous animals like electric eels, venomous snakes of all kinds, anacondas, and jaguars. They had to battle pests, disease and countless insect bites including botflies that burrow into flesh. Another issue was cutaneous leishmaniasis, a flesh-eating parasite. They had their hands full every step of the way.

After reaching the coordinates the team found a partially buried saucer shaped UFO with two dead very small occupants, undoubtedly the "grays". They also discovered various strange equipment as well as a cockpit with very odd instrumentation. They took a lot of photos and tried to gather whatever samples and small unknown equipment to bring out for analysis. The two dead occupants were nothing more that skeletons, so they also packed up some of their bones for analysis as well. There was no way to get the entire craft back due to the harsh environment and no way to haul heavy loads of any kind. The trek back to the river where they had left their boats was grueling and time-consuming, it was as if they had never cut a path through there the jungle grew back that fast. Why was the craft in the Amazon? Did it crash? The team had many unanswered questions. However, they had gathered a lot of information and future research data and items to analyze. Back in the USA, the entire project was suddenly taken over by the military and then highly classified with little to no public news releases.

There was a lot of constant and severe mental and emotional stress on all team members, the intense frustration and depression of the trip was difficult. The team relied on several GPS units to keep from getting lost in the Amazon Basin. The constant rain and severe flooding often submerged the jungle floor forcing the team to wade through miles of flooded forest. The expedition turned into a ycarlong trck to just get back to civilization.

.

Chapter Twelve:

A Haunted Farmer's Barn

Samuel Climent and his wife Rose owned a wonderful Nebraska farm home that was highly productive for his large family, he had seven children. All of the kids had specific chores and contributed to its success. However, his barn was something the whole family stayed away from at night. They all thought It was haunted, it was okay during the day but as soon as the sun went down no one ventured close to the barn.

Samuel could not understand why his barn was so strange. The farm had been in his family for many years and had a rich history of settlers looking for a better life as they passed through Sam's farm, headed west. The Oregon Trail was not far from his barn. Many pioneers from that era of American history were heading west after the Civil War to start a new life and to forget the horrors of brother killing brother. Maybe there were malevolent spirits following the settlers west and some of them were still in his barn. His grandfather often told stories of how wagon trains of all sizes would come through the farm, many even camped on the farm's pastures and rolling hills and fished in the nearby small creek that ran through the farm.

Some nights a strange light was seen shining from the barn. The horses did not like being in the barn and made it known as they were unsaddled, some even raised up on their hind legs in protest. This night the light was again seen shining from the back of the barn, there were no electric outlets in the barn, so what was this light?

During the night, the family would often hear strange noises, sounds of clanking chains and uncanny low-pitched howls and moans. The families dogs in the house would often start barking at night facing the barn with the hair on their backs standing up in alarm as if someone was there. One night the family heard what sounded like a trumpet charge used for battle, other nights they would often hear what sounded like taps being played at a funeral! Some nights Sam swore he could heard gun shots and the sound of men shouting like a battle was ensuing. Perhaps some of Sam's civil war artifacts in the house was a source? He had a .58 caliber mini ball and a .69 caliber musket ball and photos from civil war reenactments. Were these artifacts and photos calling up spirits from the Civil War?

Sam and his family were all good Christians supporting his local Baptist church. He also had acquired some questionable artifacts in his many military deployments in the U.S. and around the world. He also got rid of any items that looked like they were a part of the occult and donated them to a local museum. He donated the Civil War items as well to the local museum. He also had his minister come and pray over his home and especially the barn. He made sure that the name of Jesus Christ was mentioned and asked for God to inhabit not only his home but the barn and all of his buildings. He asked that the Lord post warrior angels around his farm and property and to protect it from any demonic powers or unclean spirits. He asked all of this in the name of Jesus Christ.

Sam was convinced that there had been evil spirits still lurking around the farm that were somehow tortured souls that may have been a part of the pioneer wagon trains that had made their way down the Oregon Trail and had found a sanctuary in his barn for some strange reason.

Suddenly the barn and entire farm became peaceful. All of the noises and strange sounds left the barn. His horses could now be bed down there. Sam still taught the Civil War as part of his local college but now had a new appreciation for what our country went through and gave thanks in prayer for the country and asked for guidance for the future. He was now even more aware and appreciative of the power of prayer and blessings.

Sam was now even more convinced that our country indeed does have a very strong Judeo-Christian background with a strong freedom of religious choice that emanates from our founding fathers principles. He also stressed that all of his students read and understand the Constitution and Bill of Rights. While not founded as a specific Christian nation the U.S. has deeply influenced Judeo-Christian values.

Malvern Hill Reenactment of battle that took place in Henrico County, Virgina. Center view is of a .69 caliber musket ball, next to it is a one-ounce lead .58 caliber mini ball.

Chapter Thirteen:

A Civil War Belt Buckle

Zak just wanted to stop in for a quick beer at the local Plum Creek, Nebraska tavern, he always thought the name the owner, Gabe, had given the bar was quite funny, "Tappy Spirits". Everyone in the little trail town of Plum Creek often stopped by the "Tappy Spirits" when convenient, for a quick brew, even some of the town's women were seen there occasionally. This was the main gathering point for town meetings. The Civil War had only been over for a short year, but the pain remained for the town and entire country, everyone in Plum Creek just wanted to forget that war and move on with their lives.

Zak had been a part of that awful war, he didn't want to talk about it, but he wore a belt buckle he had fashioned out of silver commemorating the memory of his lost Civil War friends, his handiwork often sparked comments and questions by strangers at the bar when he stopped by for a brew. The towns folks knew better than to ask Zak anything about his buckle. They all could see the pain in his eyes when asked anything about his belt

 buckle. He wore it all the time, he didn't ever want to forget his lost buddies or his close friend it commemorated.

Zak had designed the buckle using a large chunk of silver he had in his workshop. He was quite a silversmith, and his skill was used extensively by his commanders in the Civil War. His belt buckle design was a simple silhouette of a bugler, one of his best friends, Saul, had been the unit's bugler until he was tragically lost in the Battle of the Wilderness fought in Virginia in May of 1864. Saul was from a small town in Alabama named Eufaula.

One sultry day Zak was having a beer at the Tappy Spirits bar when a stranger asked him about the buckle he wore. Somehow the stranger looked familiar to Zak, he asked the stranger why he was asking, the bearded and disheveled stranger said he had been in the Civil War but had traveled to Nebraska to get as far away as he could to forget all those awful war memories, especially the Wilderness War battle where he was wounded. When Zak asked him his name the stranger said it was Chill and then the memories flooded over Zak's mind, he knew Chill from General Grant's Overland Campaign, he had met him briefly in one of the hastily assembled battlefield tent hospitals when the doctors were trying to save his friend Saul's life, Chill was then, what Zak thought one of the doctors in the tent, this painful memory seemed so long ago. They had hastily moved Saul to a nearby farmers' barn that was serving as a makeshift hospital, but Saul passed away before the doctors could do anything to save him. Zak just wanted to forget that whole awful war memory and besides that Chill's appearance was that of an old man who didn't take very good care of himself. Zak didn't hesitate to ask him, "What the "hell" has happened to you Chill, it's been over a year since the war ended?"

Chill was reluctant to speak for a moment but then with his head bowed down he began to reluctantly explain his situation. He said, "Working as a doctor's aide in the battlefield tents, I saw so much carnage, suffering and death, it was so heart breaking and stressful, more so than I realized." He continued, "So after the war I returned home to Montgomery, Alabama to my family, my parents didn't even recognize me at first as I approached the home farm. All I wanted to do was get back to working the fields and settling down to some kind of normal." My mother Isabella was so shocked at my frail appearance she immediately began trying to feed me several times a day, my father finally told her to just settle down and let me relax and get used to being home again in Alabama. My old girlfriend, Martha had finally married when no one had heard from me, all my friends and family thought I was dead and had been lost in the war. I saw Martha in town one day and she didn't even recognize me when I said hello, she was totally shocked when I introduced myself, she didn't recognize me and my appearance didn't help. She was very hesitant to even talk much, she said she was now married so I asked her who she married, it was one of my old friends Able. I was amazed she had married him, he was a very poor student and was not able to serve in the war due to some of his medical conditions. I told her to give him my regards as she left the store where I saw her.

Zak's belt buckle continued to spark many discussions and questions by those in the bar that had never seen the buckle before. Zak at one time briefly thought he should just quit wearing it, but he could not for many reasons.

One day Zak got letter from Saul's little sister Mara who lived in Magnolia Springs, Alabama. He was shocked, he didn't remember her at all and never remembered Saul ever saying anything about having a sister, the letter said she was Saul's little sister and when he left for the war she was only two years old, so she doesn't remember him at all. In her letter, she hoped she could get Zak to tell her more about her older brother Saul. Mara had just found Zak's address in some of Saul's old family papers; she hoped Zak's address was still good. She said she didn't know much about her brother and her parents were reluctant to tell her much, they were so heart broken when Saul never returned from the war, they didn't want to talk much about him at all.

Zak got out some paper and his pen but just didn't really know how to start the letter. How could he even begin to painfully write about his best friend so his little sister would know more about him? Just the thought of writing a letter about Saul overwhelmed Zak's mind so painfully, but he knew this letter had to be written, not only for Mara but for Zak himself as well. In trying to rationalize this task, he thought this would be a way for him to begin to deal more responsibly with the loss of his best friend in this horrible war between the states.

Zak started the letter stating Saul was one highly respected and funny guy who had everyone laughing and he was also, besides a talented bugler, a crack shot and marksman. Everyone liked Saul and thought very highly of him. He also wore his uniform proudly and was impeccable in his dress uniform. Zak also had saved a couple of tin type photos of Saul in his uniform, so he was going to include one with the letter to his sister Mara.

Zak didn't want to tell Mara too much about the bloody Virginia battle except it took place in a dense, tangled fire prone forest in early May, many of the soldiers who died were wounded and trapped in the heavy under brush. He wanted to stress that many reported seeing Saul rescuing wounded soldiers who were trapped in the burning forest. General Ulysses S. Grant said of Saul, one of his buglers, that he was indeed one of the heroes of Wilderness Battle and that he had saved many soldiers' lives that day.

Saul also included one tin type photograph of two of them standing together proudly in their uniforms, the best of friends. Saul said that he hoped to meet Mara in person someday.

Chapter Fourteen:

The Lone Scream?

It was a blustery fall day in the little town of Hardyville. The town was growing too rapidly for many of the old timers, but it was right on the main trail west that all of the old wagon trains used back in the early 1860's on their way to California. The main street looked like one of the old towns used in the old western movies and in fact one western movie had been filmed there years ago. That part of the town was being historically preserved as the more modern additions were being built all around that part of the downtown. The town was becoming a thriving small modern city.

Located near the edge of town was an old abandoned three story home many said was haunted, no one wanted to buy it, so it just languished there. Not even the kids wanted to visit the house or play near the font entry gate, it truly looked like something out of an old Halloween movie. The city was continually after the owner, a distant family cousin to keep it cleaned up or sell it, but the owner Old Seraphim Gabby Grayson was a cantankerous guy and hard to talk to about the old house or any of his real estate holdings in the town. Old Gabby, as everyone called him, did keep it in some semblance of repair, it needed to be repainted, and he did keep the grounds half way maintained and mowed.

No power was connected to the old house; however, it was completely wired for electricity, and it had been functioning in the past when the house was occupied by the famous local family from Scotland the famous Whitney Langley Selkirk-Armstrong, who had made his fortune in his famous Kirkcaldy Scotch Whiskey Distilleries. The old man Whitney lived to be 95 years old and passed away quietly in that old mansion at the end of town. He had owned thousands of acres around the house, some of it had been sold for the town's golf course but most of it lay empty and undeveloped. Old Gabby owned it all but would not sell any of it as he was approached many times by real estate developers.

There was a huge stone wall around the house with an imposing entry gate that was now rusting and was always open. There was a winding road to the house. It had been reported that on certain nights there could be seen a woman standing in the window above the main entrance dressed in white with the room dimly lighted, strange as the power had long ago been shut off to the house. That was supposedly the bedroom of Whitney's wife Salome Vendetta Armstrong who had mysteriously disappeared many years ago. Rumors swirled around her that she was just as eccentric as her husband and that she had mysteriously died there and was buried somewhere on the property. There was a family cemetery on the property with headstones listing who were buried there. There was one grave with a large statue above it of a woman, that grave was unmarked. Stories had circulated that Salome was buried there as it had her birthdate engraved on it but no date of death or name of induvial buried there if anyone had even been buried there at all. Stories had circulated that Salome was tortured and murdered by Old Gabby in the house. Of course there was no proof of this, only rumors.

A team of real estate developers were visiting and wanted to see the house. They also toured the property and were developing plans for a large community to be built there complete with a large mall. They were in negotiations with Old Gabby. The small team of three real estate developers were staying in a RV that was parked near the front gate of the old house.

The last night they were to stay there they all saw the strange women in white standing in the window and were alarmed, not only by what they were seeing but there was also a severe storm warning in the local weather forecast with high winds, lightening and heavy rain possible.

During the midst of the storm, they all could plainly see the strange woman in the window when suddenly there was a blood curdling scream coming from the house just as a bolt of lightning struck the old mansion. The house immediately erupted into flames and burned to the ground. As the police and fire fighters sifted through the wreckage they found two skeletons, one was identified using DNA as Old Gabby. The other skeleton was that of a woman. Was this indeed the body of the long-missing Salome Vendetta Armstrong? The DNA results indicated that the woman was indeed a family member.

Locals say it was the ghost of Salome Vendetta Armstrong that was seen in the window, and the house was destroyed as retribution for all the pain she had suffered there.

Apparently, Salome's body had been in the house somewhere for years. Old Gabby had often stayed in the house in one of the bedrooms. The police report said he died in the fire. No one was aware that he had been staying there the night of the storm.

Chapter Fifteen:

Grandma's Attic AM-FM Radio

Seth loved to visit his grandma Tate, she was one cool lady and had so many stories to tell of her early life growing up in Nebraska. Seth made a point to visit his grandmother when he could, she now lived alone in the old family farm home at the edge of town. She had so many interesting stories of her farm life in a small town named Oconto, Nebraska. That town no longer exists, in its place now is nothing but farmland with a few old buildings here and there.

One Saturday afternoon she told Seth he could go upstairs into the attic and see if there was anything he might be interested in having, he was shocked as that was always the one place she had forbidden anyone to enter. He excitedly went up the dusty staircase into the attic and began looking around at all the really old historic memorabilia she had stored there, his eye caught an old AM/FM radio. Seth was the only one in his class at school who even knew what the old radios were and how they worked, everyone his age was always looking down at their cell phones. None of his friends knew anything about how the cell phones even worked, he did thanks to his grandpa Orva who was an old electronics engineer. He and his grandpa loved history and spent lots of time just talking about all the wonderful Nebraska history. Sadly, Grandpa Orva passed a couple of years ago leaving Grandma Tate now alone.

He quickly dusted off the radio case, he was surprised it looked so good, it looked like it was a brand-new radio. Grandma's old saying that they don't make things like they used to sure seems to apply here. He plugged in the radio and turned it on, of course it didn't work, he wasn't surprised. Also, in the attic Seth found his grandpa's old

tube tester next to a box of old tubes. He knew what they were as his grandpa had spent time teaching him how to test the tubes used in the old radios if they didn't work. Seth got out the old tube tester and plugged it in and to his surprise it worked so he went about testing each tube. The ones that didn't work he tossed aside and luckily he found replacement tubes for the radio in his grandpa's old tube box. After he had replaced three tubes he plugged in the radio again and to his amazement it seemed to be working, he could hear some static and humming noises coming from the radio's speaker. As he turned the dial he soon picked up all the local AM stations, he was excited that Grandma Tate's radio was now working.

He turned over to the FM side, and it too was working. His grandpa had taken the time to explain to Seth the difference between amplitude modulation (AM) and Frequency Modulation (FM) used in early radio programming in the 1930's and 40's. As Seth turned the dial it suddenly just stopped at 108.1. Seth thought that was strange, no FM radio stations he knew about had a frequency above 107.9. What was even stranger, the old radio had a 108.1 marked on its dial, however it did not light up unless the radio was turned on, when off or unplugged no 108.1 showed up on the dial! Seth was getting confused and a bit frightened. Why did that frequency only show up when the radio was on?

Then a voice from the radio mysteriously said, "Hey Seth, how are you doing!" The voice was so clear it startled Seth for a moment, and it was very familiar sounding. After a short pause, the voice said, "This is your uncle Benjamin." Seth knew immediately who he was, it was his favorite Uncle! Uncle Ben was a WWII hero having been in the U.S. Army serving in Germany at the end of the second World War.

"Seth, Seth, wake up you are having a bad dream." It was his mom Imma shaking him awake. "It's time for you to get up, get a move on or you will be late to your 7:30 am college International Relations class."

Seth was shaking nervously and drenched in sweat, he told his mother he was having a bad dream about the old radio grandma Tate gave him. All he could think about was hearing his Uncle Ben's voice coming from the radio's speaker.

Later that day after classes, Seth reluctantly turned on the old radio, it was working well but as he looked at it the dial on FM 107.9, it was bright red, the other numbers were in a dim white light. He continued to use the radio all through his college days and never had the dream again but the light on 107.9 was always red for some unknown and unexplainable reason and a stark reminder of his terrifying dream.

Chapter Sixteen:

Arizona's Flying Monster – Really?

It's April of 1890 and Elam is just a few miles west of Tombstone, Arizona and as always, he is alone on the trail. Nothing seems to bother him, but this sound he is hearing is like something out of a nightmare. The old cowboy pulled his rifle out of its leather scabbard as he sat restlessly in the saddle. What in the world was that awful sound he was hearing? He has never heard anything quite so terrifying, it can't be a mountain lion. It's a bone curdling howling growl-like scream. Elam has to find a place to set up camp soon as the sun is slowly setting, but first he has to check out this unknown animal sound. He is not sure where it is coming from.

Elam is not only a cowboy but a talented writer. He had worked for the Tombstone Epitaph for a short time but missed the wide-open spaces so signed up as a range cowboy with the large Henry Hooker Sierra Bonita ranch, one of Arizona's largest ranches. His job tonight is to check on some of Hooker's cattle grazing north of his ranch. While camping, Elam would sometimes get his pad and paper out and jot down a short story or two before his camp fire went out and his mind faded into a deep sleep. He always said sleeping under the stars in the open was very restful and that was when he would indulge his vivid imagination and write short stories. Elam could not get a decent night of rest in the wild raucous Arizona towns. He always preferred sleeping under the stars anyway.

However, this night was strangely different, even the insects and howling coyotes were quiet, the lack of any sound along with the blood curdling howling and growling scream had unnerved Elam. Who or what was out there that had silenced the sounds of nature? The night settled down as Elam stoked his camp fire. He rolled out his bedding as the stars shown down brightly. The sounds of nature had returned. He never knew what that horrible scream was or where it came from, his sleep was restless this night.

The next morning Elam wondered if he had indeed heard Tombstone's mythical winged monster. He remembered one of the Epitaph's newspaper reports recently about two ranchers who supposedly shot and killed a large, 18-foot winged creature of some kind in the high desert. No one knew if this was true or where the creature was buried. Elam was aware of the Navajo Indians mythology about colossal Thunderbirds who protected nature and were revered by the tribe. Elam had done some research into this cryptid flying creature that had been reported over the years but not scientifically researched or named. Was this what he had heard?

Elam wondered could there still be a living pterodactyl out there somewhere in Arizona? Elam reasoned that could be impossible as the Pterodactyl went extinct over 60 million years ago, or did it? Perhaps there is a gateway or a wormhole that allows prehistoric creatures to access Earth, which is just as preposterous as a flying pterodactyl monster still living in the rugged Arizona territories! Just what did he hear and what have others really seen in past reports of this strange large flying creature? Elam was determined to find out somehow.

Paleontologists have discovered the remains of one of the oldest known pterosaur fossils in North America in Arizona's Petrified Forest National Park located in between Flagstaff and the New Mexico border. Despite all of the claims over the years of people seeing these large unknown bird-like creatures they have never been photographed. Cryptozoologists have speculated there may indeed be a living pterodactyl out there while others think many of these so-called sightings are nothing but fabricated tall tales. Talk to any Navajo historian or tribal leader and most firmly believe in the colossal and powerful Thunderbirds. They are powerful and very destructive monsters that were defeated by the Navajo tribe in the mythical past. So, the question has to be asked, are these actual reports fact or not?

Elam set out to try and devise a plan using the new portable box camera invented in 1888, of course they didn't work at night, so it was nearly impossible to somehow capture evidence of these large mysterious flying creatures using the cumbersome glass plate negatives so that idea wouldn't work. He first had to research just what all of these past reports have in common, time of day of sightings, any particular time of the year and any other similar perinate data surrounding the sightings. He would also seek out those individuals and get first hand reports if possible for those willing to relate they actually saw a flying monster.

After months of interviews and camping at night in areas of reported sightings and other various times during the day, Elam had nothing much to report. His efforts were turning into a colossal waste of his time.

After several months of assembling reports Elam found that many of the sightings are at night, near sunset or pre-dawn hours. The reports all indicate the large creature looked like a winged reptile with skin covered wings not covered in feathers. The reports often indicate they are shining varying in colors from red, blue, green, or yellow. The reports also say the creature has a reptile's head on a long neck with a ferocious looking mouth as well as a long tail.

Another fact Elam was considering concerned the late 1800s mining industry in southern Arizona. Many had left the little dusty town of Tombstone so any exciting news story for the newspaper to report was a major challenge as the population was declining so rapidly. So, what better way to excite the town and sell newspapers than a monster story? One very old cowboy even reported he was actually one of the ranchers that shot at the strange creature and chased it, they were quite frightened but never shot it down. The old timer also said the horses were so spooked and wouldn't respond so they gave up the chase.

The story of the Tombstone Thunderbird is now an Arizona legend. Many reports through the years indicated many people supposedly remembered seeing the picture in magazines and newspapers but that really is not a possibility as the Tombstone Epitaph and newspapers in the 1800s had no ability to publish pictures. Interestingly, the Library of Congress has the issue of the Tombstone Epitaph from April of 1890 and of course there is no photo, so the legend continues.

Chapter Seventeen:

Ned the Old Nebraska Cowboy

Ned was getting his horse out of the barn and preparing to head out north to the edge of his property that bordered the Nebraska Sand Hills when a huge flock of Sandhill Cranes started circling to land near a pond not far from his farm house. The Cranes were on their way back to central Canada and farther north. They wouldn't be staying long after their winter stay in the south was over.

Those birds always mystified Ned, such big, beautiful creatures, and such great flyers. So many large, amazing birds and they never collide with each other in flight. Another of God's amazing creations.

The Sandhill Cranes distracted Ned, he really wanted to check out the strange noise he heard in the middle of the night. It was as if he was in the big city and not out in the rolling sandhills of his ranch. It sounded like a car crash.

He saddled up his favorite horse, "Partner" because it had the uncanny ability to sense things, the strange crashing noise had unnerved all of his stock as he could hear them most of the night howling and milling about in the pasture next to the barn. However, Partner was quite calm as they moved out toward the pasture west of the barn. As Ned came around a grove of Eastern Red Cedar

 trees he had planted as a wind break he could see what looked like a shining piece of aluminum sticking out of the sandy soil. Ned had been an intelligence analyst in the Air Force, so he had developed a high level of observational skills and quickly assessed this as a possible crashed aircraft.

Ned's horse Partner wouldn't go near the area. As he got off his horse and walked over to the crash site, he could see what looked like an aircraft of some kind partially buried. He could see a hatch that was partly open. When he looked inside he was startled, he could clearly see two small gray colored bodies of the occupants, one was sitting at a strange consol of instruments Ned had never seen before, the other was slumped over on the side of the craft, he thought to himself, "This must be the navigator." Ned was a key volunteer in the local Unidentified Aeriel Phenomena Task Force (UAPTF) and also served as a deputy sheriff. Aerial Phenomena Task Force had been started by the old

Department of Defense (DOD) now called the Department of War (DOW). Ned's first reaction was to report this to his law enforcement chain of command, but he also realized this could start an unwelcome rush of media to his ranch and local community, but he reasoned it has to be done so he quickly got on the phone and reported what he had found. He had just finished his verbal report when the phone rang again, this time it was from his good friend and fellow task force member, Joe Barnaby who was also a deputy sheriff.

Joe said, *"Hey Ned my man what is going on out at your ranch? I could see a lot of strange lights over your way Ned!"* Joe lived in the next section to the west of Ned and had a large number of cattle on his ranch. Joe's ranch covered over two sections and was over 1500 acres. To answer Joe's question, Ned proceeded to fill Joe in with all the details. Joe said he would be right out to take down the information since Joe also wrote the small newspaper for the area residents. Joe would try and keep the media as uniformed and out of the way as he could, but the media is always monitoring the local radio frequencies so undoubtedly the media would be headed out toward the ranch as well if they thought something strange was going on since there had been sightings of strange flying objects reported in the past. Ned knew the media all too well and that this was going to happen, but he had a responsibility to keep law enforcement informed so they could investigate this phenomenon.

Ned decided to stay up the next night and see if he would see anything strange again flying above his ranch. Everything was calm as the night wore on, there was no moon this night, so it was very dark as the sky was filled with stars. He was keeping his eye on the area where the UFO had crashed and about midnight he could hear a strange humming sound and then suddenly he saw a huge saucer shaped craft slowly descending, he had never seen anything that large before as it slowly hovered over his ranch. What he saw next was nothing but amazing, the

 crashed UFO began to slowly rise up and was swallowed into the center of the larger circular craft. Then just as suddenly as it appeared it shot straight up and disappeared into the dark night sky.

The next morning early, Ned raced out to the area of the crashed UFO, all that was left was a large hole where it had crashed. As he investigated the area, he noticed a metallic fragment protruding out of the sandy soil. As Ned examined the fragment, he found it to be quite different, he could bend and fold it like a piece of paper and it would return to its original shape after left in its folded and bent situation for few minutes. He wondered aloud, "What is this strange metal."

Ned also noted that his metal wrist band he wore that contained his watch and a compass, he noticed the compass was spinning like a top, what kind of strange electromagnetic disturbance would cause his compass to go crazy? Ned's horse Partner would not go near the area and stayed away often raring up as Ned road up to the area, he almost threw Ned off, so what was it the horse was detecting?

About that time, Joe in his Jeep drove up to the area. Joe began photographing the area and taking notes as Ned talked about what he had witnessed. Joe was as equally amazed as well as Ned at what had happened. Joe said he wondered now what kind of story the U.S. government investigators would make up to explain away this UFO incident. There's no swamps and swamp gas in Taylor's high desert region! At the bottom of the metal fragment in small print was a strange caption that made no sense, almost like an imprint of who and what made this metallic-like piece of the unidentified aerial phenomenon (UAP) craft:

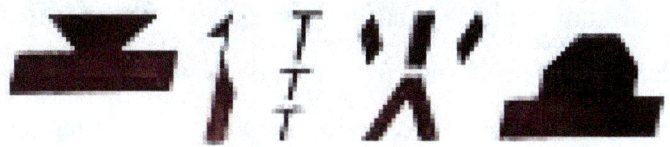

On the backside of the metal fragment Ned noticed this imprinted symbol.

As soon as all of this information was released to law enforcement, Ned's ranch was overwhelmed with Federal agents who immediately seized the metal alien fragments. They also confiscated all of Joe's notes and camera, however, Joe had emailed all of his notes and photos to himself in his very private email he only used for personal family contacts. So at least there was a record of

what had happened even though it would all be censored, denied, and changed by the U.S. government as they continue to suppress all UFO/UAP data collected by civilians. The question has to asked why is the U.S. government suppressing UFO/UAP data?

Ned's community, Taylor, Nebraska was already quite well known locally and in the state as the home of the early pioneer cut outs a local artist, Marah Sandoz, had erected all over town. Taylor, Nebraska is a village and in the county seat of Loup County, Nebraska, United States. ("Taylor, Nebraska - Wikipedia") The population was 190 in the 2010 census. Taylor was laid out and platted in 1883 and was named for Ed Taylor, a pioneer settler in the area.

The artist, Marah Sandoz says, "I never set out to make a name for myself as an artist." She adds, "I want as many wooden people as there are actual people in Taylor, which is only 182." Marah's husband, Loren Sandoz is related to Nebraska-born and famous writer Mari Sandoz. Her husband was a local teacher who brought Marah to Taylor. About 20 years ago she got involved with a local economic development group brainstorming ways to help the fading village of Taylor get more attention, Taylor is right on the edge of the picturesque and locally famous Sandhills. The economic group was seeking ways to use the local history of Taylor's two historic buildings, the closed Pavilion Hotel and a former filling station, turned into a local visitors center, sitting on the two state highways that intersected in the town. How could the economic group turn this history into Taylor's advantage? Besides being on the route of the famous annual 300-mile "Nebraska Junk Jaunt" celebrating a continuous yard sale in the center of Nebraska that is always held in late September.

The economic brainstorming session decided to go back to Taylor's past history, one of the ideas was Marah's wooden recreation of those famous 1890 Taylor citizens. Marah used her skill in creating wooden people in cutouts that depicted people living in Tayor between 1890 and 1920, Taylor's boom years.

The first two wooden villagers created by Marah were put on display in 2003 named "Herbert and Alice" standing near the old Pavilion Hotel and then "Ralph and Hank" chatting by the visitors center. Locals thought they were fun Marah said. They were different, so people said they had to stop and wait as they thought they were people wanting to cross the street. Some locals even waved at them, so the cutouts created a lot of local chatter.

The cutouts became Marah's project since she was a self-trained artist with experience in using wood and paint, her "people" depicted Taylor citizens who might have lived in that era. The wooden populace draws visitors and stops those passing through on the highway to enjoy the cutouts and local businesses like the *Bootleg Brewers* offering craft beers and *Marah's Treasures*, a local popular art shop that offers custom-made cutouts and a variety of other art.

So, not only the Sandhills of the area is an attraction but now the little village of Taylor sitting on the edge of the

Sandhills. If planning a trip through Nebraska put the Sandhills and Taylor on your travel agenda. The Sandhills area is a vast ecological region in north-central Nebraska known for their grass-covered and stabilized sand dunes.

During your trip and stay in the sandhills region you might also be fortunate enough to see a UFO or two flying over and checking out the famous Sandhills of Nebraska. Stop by the *Bootleg Brewers* for a quick beer and if you are lucky you might get a chance to talk to some of the local cattle ranchers, perhaps you will hear some more stories about UFOs seen in Taylor, Nebraska.

Chapter Eighteen:

Tiras and His "Spacetime" Venture into an Unknown Dimension

Tiras knew the invisible energy spreading out over the space craft would be hard to eliminate, his speed was now approaching the actual speed of light, so he was getting nervous. His ship was now entering into an unknown region of space and time. Was Albert Einstein correct about time? His theory was that space and time are not separate at all but somehow interwoven into a multi-dimensional reality he called "Spacetime." Tiras was about to find out.

Tiras was a highly decorated Space Federation test pilot. He knew this was a dangerous test flight only to travel to the outer limits of our solar system for a brief research orbit of the planet Neptune using the new hyperdrive anti gravitational propulsion system. The speed was not to exceed what the astrophysicists had indicated was approximately one quarter the speed of light or 46,500 miles per second. Neptune was 3 billion miles from Earth so it would take 18 hours to reach the planet at one quarter the speed of light. Tiras had lost control of the hyperdrives complex internal antigravitational regulators, they would not respond as his speed just increased past all known previous speed test flights. He had feared his ship would break up or just simply disintegrate at the speed he was approaching neared the actual speed of light. The strange colorful tunnel he had entered was an unknown result of his speed.

He thought was this some kind of strange "spacetime energy" he was now experiencing? It was now engulfing his entire space ship. The ship began to take on a different hue and color as his speed increased. His instrument panel was flashing red warning lights, the entire ship was shaking, Tiras for a moment thought he might not make it through this harrowing encounter with this unpredictable "spacetime" high speed test.

The view of outer space looked like a bright red and blue tunnel affair; his ship was speeding toward the center bright light. As he entered the light his ship suddenly came to stop; his instruments indicated he was in the Constellation Centaurus.

As suddenly as it all started his ship now was quiet except for the sound of the air conditioning and life support equipment. His instruments also indicated he was now orbiting the exoplanet Proxima Centauri b. His automated flight control systems were working well.

Previous long distant sensor-based research had also indicated there was a possible habitable zone on the planet. Tiras thought to himself, this is impossible, the Constellation Centaurus is 4.24 light years away from Earth. What kind of a "spacetime" tunnel had he entered due to his speed? Our sun is the closest star to Earth, the next closest star to Earth is Proxima Centauri, so how did he suddenly get over 4 light years away from

Earth so quickly? His big worry now was, how could he return to Earth or was it now impossible? He was indeed experiencing uncharted and unexpected results of this speed test.

Tiras had been inadvertently sucked into what Artificial Intelligence (AI) had discovered existing as a low-density high-temperature channel of plasma that connected our solar system toward the Centaurus Constellation. The higher temperature of the plasma channel must be what caused Tiras' controls to not respond and then coupled with the high speed, he thought to himself, he was lucky to still be alive. Had Tiras inadvertently discovered how to now traverse the immensity of spacetime using this plasma channel as a hyperspace wormhole?

The Proxima b planet looked brown as compared to the blue planet of Earth. As he examined the planet he could see isolated areas that

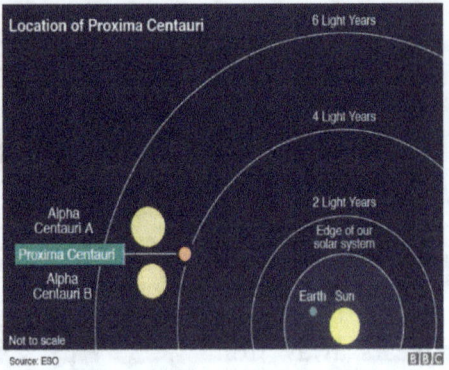

looked like some kind of growth and some areas even appeared to have what looked like water to some degree. However, what was strangest were gigantic dinosaur like animals and other reptile-looking creatures roaming about the planet. There indeed seemed to be a wide range of very different life that had evolved there. He could not see anything that looked like humanoids, but he was not going to stay long enough to find out. He was only equipped for a test flight, not any exploration. Tiras engaged every type of sensor he had to record what he was seeing. He decided not to get any type of samples for fear of how they might react to Earth's climate and what they might harbor that could be dangerous. Indeed, the life there seemed to be thriving but did not appear to be water based like Earth's carbon type vegetative plant life using photosynthesis to thrive.

Tiras next checked how much of his Di-lithium crystals were left to power up his special antigravitational engine in his attempt to return to Earth and in the right time frame. He calculated he could just reverse his course using the same headings and procedures. There were plenty of Di-lithium crystals for the return flight.

After all systems were ready he engaged his hyperspace drive to reverse his course and return to Earth. Everything was set up and ready as he engaged his hyperspace drive. Just as suddenly as it all began he was in a flash of time back in his own solar system, his instruments indicated he was in the right time frame as well.

He received a message from space command flight control and asked what had happened, his ship just suddenly disappeared from their tracking radar. Tiras asked how long was he gone, command flight control said he was gone for a full fifteen minutes. He said this test flight had gathered a lot of sensor information and looked forward to the assessment and evaluation of more data than could be imagined and told them his flight debriefing would be simply unbelievable along with supportive photographic and radar data.

Chapter Nineteen:

Is Archimedes Fire Possibly a Myth?

Archimedes was born approximately in 287BC in the city of Syracuse, located on the island of Sicily. He was the son of an astronomer named Phidias. Archimedes was a mathematician and inventor and spent most of his life in his hometown except for a noted visit to  Alexandria in Egypt. His death was recorded to have taken place when a Roman soldier was sent to capture him and in the middle of determining a geometry proof drawn in the sand on his floor, Archimedes supposedly said to the Roman "Do not disturb my diagrams." The soldier flew into a rage and beat the 75-year-old genius to death. ("What was Archimedes' death ray? - HowStuffWorks") According to history, Archimedes' war machines kept the Romans at bay, and many historians indicate his death ray was particularly effective.

In the ancient world bitumen was a dark sticky petroleum-based chemical often used to water proof boats and ships. And while there is no evidence Archimedes had used it in his design of war devices, but it is entirely possible he did use it or list it as a possible war fighting material in his war machine designs.

It is entirely possible that Archimedes used a series of giant mirrors in his so-called death ray. He well could have used not only these mirrors in battle but along with the distraction of the light from the mirrors invaders could also have launched flammable tar balls and other projectiles. What really happened is lost in the fog of time.

The Archimedes steam cannon from the third century B.C. functioned with steam and was designed to be in a cylindrical metal boiler with a wooden barrel to launch stone balls. The Barrel was blocked with a wooden beam and when the boiler reached the appropriate temperature in a fire the valve was opened and the water poured into the boiler, evaporated rapidly and when the wooden beam was broken the stone ball was launched by the steam.

In one testing of the Archimedes death ray, a group of Massachusetts Institute of Technology (MIT) researchers in 2005 constructed a 10-foot long one each thick red oak version of a Roman ship. As part of the research, they used 127 one-foot square flat mirrors arranged in a parabolic concave arc. After ten minutes the researchers managed to set the model ship on fire.

The problem with this test is that the ship was motionless, most ships would be rocking on the sea due to waves. The test took place in a highly controlled area as have other tests bringing into doubt the actual event having ever taken place. Many other tests have also resulted in mixed results at best. Most likely this tale of using mirrors against the Romans is a myth.

One other test of note was conducted in 1973 when a Greek engineer undertook his own experiment when he had 70 soldiers each holding 5-foot by 3-foot mirrors reflecting the sunlight. The concentrated beam set a row boat 160 feet off the shore aflame.

Other researches have also wondered if it had been so effective a weapon why weren't these mirrors added to the armaments of those times? As more tests emerge in the future and the reality of Archimedes' death ray is disproven, it will have little effect on detracting from his genius.

Many historians don't even mention Archimedes' use of mirrors when discussing the Roman siege of Syracuse that took place in 213-212 BC. It is entirely likely that if mirrors had been used they would have been a major distraction for the Roman army hampering and slowing its final victory over Syracuse.

For historic events involving Archimedes that took place so long ago, it is a challenge to find accurate verification due to the stories getting changed and embellished as they are retold and included in ancient historic documentations. What really happened often turns into myth.

Archimedes contributions in mathematics, physics and engineering has resulted in a whole host of practical devices our modern world takes for granted. Many historians have the opinion he was born out of place in history, his concepts, theories, and abilities were indeed centuries ahead of his time in the ancient world.

Bibliography

Blacksmith-Ncolonial-Blacksmiths-Minutemen-Revolutionar. (n.d.). Retrieved from https://www.amazon.com/Blacksmith-Ncolonial-Blacksmiths-Minutemen-Revolutionary/dp/B07CG8G6RZ

News-articles/can-wooden-people-bring-life-to-taylor-nebraska. (n.d.). Retrieved from https://nebraskapublicmedia.org/en/news/news-articles/can-wooden-people-bring-life-to-taylor-nebraska/

Time-slips-the-multiverse-and-you. (n.d.). Retrieved from https://www.psychologytoday.com/us/blog/where-physics-meets-psychology/202201/time-slips-the-multiverse-and-you

www.ingramcontent.com/pod-product-compliance
Lightning Source LLC
Chambersburg PA
CBHW071532100726
47908CB00004B/1368